This igloo book belongs to:

Evie Welsh 9¾ nearley 10p6

No 3 - No 5

igloobooks

Published in 2014
by Igloo Books Ltd
Cottage Farm
Sywell
NN6 0BJ
www.igloobooks.com

SHE001 0114
2 4 6 8 10 9 7 5 3
ISBN 978-1-78197-154-3

© Dissero Brands Limited (New Zealand) 2013
All worldwide rights reserved.
www.rachaelhale.com

Printed and manufactured in China

Kitten Tales

igloobooks

The kittens are all having lots of fun playing games. "I'm a great climber," says Eric, as he clings on to his rope swing. "Does anyone else want to climb with me?"

"No, thank you," purrs Tinker. "I prefer to play with my big ball of wool. It is so soft and best of all, it's pink." Tinker likes to wrap the cosy wool around her like a woolly blanket.

Lizzy loves playing hide-and-seek.
She always finds the best hiding places.
"Aha! This will be a purr-fect place," thinks Lizzy.
"Mitzy will never find me in here."

Mitzy spots Lizzy hiding in the little, blue bin.
"Peek-a-boo! I see you!" she shouts, happily.
"Well done, Mitzy," laughs Lizzy. "I'll find an even
better hiding place next time."

"I've blown up a balloon so that I can play Balloon Bounce," says Mia. "I mustn't let the balloon touch the floor. I wonder if anyone else will play with me?"

"I'll play with you," says Ginger. "I just want to finish
my cupcake first. It looks so yummy!"
"Do you have any more?" asks Mia. "It looks delicious."
"Sorry, Mia. This is my last one," replies Ginger, licking his lips.

Phyllis and Jo are having fun drawing with chalk on a big blackboard. "I've drawn a beautiful crown," says Phyllis. "What have you drawn, Jo?" "I drew lots of pretty hearts," replies Jo.

Having fun is thirsty work, so Maria
is preparing a nice, cool drink for all her kitten friends.
"I'm sure that everyone will enjoy a fresh glass of milk," says Maria.

It is a bright, sunny day outside, so Poppet is playing in the garden. "The flowers all look so lovely at this time of year," she says, happily. "Perhaps I will make flower necklaces for my friends."

"That's a wonderful idea," says Lara.
"I love flower necklaces. Can you make me one, please?"
"Of course," says Poppet, laughing. "Here you are, Lara."

Honey prefers to read a good book indoors,
rather than play outside. "Books are full of wonderful stories,"
she says. "There are tales about princesses, ponies
and all sorts of pretty things."

"I love books, too," says Willow. "I like to read tales about fairies and magic. Those stories are so exciting! I wish that I could do magic, too."

Kayla has found some old clothes
in one of the cupboards upstairs
and is playing dress-up.
"With this furry scarf I look
like a famous actress!"
she cries, happily.

"We're pretending to go to a posh dinner party," say Tom and Mia. Mia is wearing a beautiful pearl necklace and Tom has found a very smart, black bow tie.

Lexie has found a sparkly handbag.
"I'm going to pretend that I'm
shopping in Paris," she says.
"I will be able to put all my new
clothes in my fancy handbag."

Oh, dear. Guiness' hat is a
little too big for him.
"Hey, who turned out the lights?"
asks Guiness, grinning.
"Oh, Guiness, you're so funny,"
laugh Lexie, Tom and Mia.

"I'm playing with the pearls
from the dressing-up box,"
says Leah.
"They are all so sparkly
and pretty."

Lily has had so much fun playing games and running around that she is feeling rather worn out. "I feel quite sleepy now," she says, with a big yawn. "Perhaps I'll have a quiet nap underneath these sweet-smelling flowers."

After playing games all day, it is now time for the kittens to go to bed. They say goodbye to each other before settling down for a lovely sleep.
Goodnight, everyone.

The kittens had lots of fun playing games together.
Are you good at games and puzzles?
See if you can answer the questions below.

1. Which little kitten loves to play with a ball of wool?

2. Lizzy has found a great hiding place. Where is it?

3. What tasty treat is Ginger about to eat?

4. What delicious drink has Mariah made for everyone?

5. What special gift has Poppet made for Lara?

6. What sort of tales does Willow like to read about?

1. Tinker 2. In a blue bin 3. A cupcake 4. Milk 5. A flower necklace 6. Fairies and magic.

Goodbye!